TURNED
EARTH

LOUISIANA STATE UNIVERSITY PRESS | BATON ROUGE

TURNED
EARTH POEMS
BRAD RICHARD

Published by Louisiana State University Press
lsupress.org

LSU Press Paperback Original

Designer: Kaelin Chappell Broaddus
Typefaces: Garamond Premier Pro, Ambrose Std, Acumin Pro Wide

Lyrics quoted in "Lapis Lazuli":
STRAWBERRY LETTER 23
Words and Music by SHUGGIE OTIS
© 1971, 1992 KIDADA MUSIC INC. and OFF THE WALL MUSIC
All Rights Administered by WARNER-TAMERLANE PUBLISHING CORP.
All Rights Reserved
Used by Permission of ALFRED MUSIC

Cover illustration: Detail of *Untitled*, 1994, by Rosalie Ramm.

Library of Congress Cataloging-in-Publication Data

Names: Richard, Brad, author.
Title: Turned earth : poems / Brad Richard.
Description: Baton Rouge : Louisiana State University Press, 2025.
Identifiers: LCCN 2024047647 (print) | LCCN 2024047648 (ebook) | ISBN
   978-0-8071-8375-5 (paperback) | ISBN 978-0-8071-8418-9 (epub) | ISBN
   978-0-8071-8419-6 (pdf)
Subjects: LCGFT: Poetry.
Classification: LCC PS3568.I299 T87 2025 (print) | LCC PS3568.I299
   (ebook) | DDC 811/.6—dc23/eng/20241021
LC record available at https://lccn.loc.gov/2024047647
LC ebook record available at https://lccn.loc.gov/2024047648

for Tim

and

in memory of my mother,
Nell Parker (1944–2015)

CONTENTS

TURNED
EARTH

HOW I AM WHOLE

Some days I just want to be an idea.
Form. Duration. *Écriture.* But my body
keeps getting me lost in things: mist

so white it brightens my classroom windows
before thickening into rain, the slow
darkening of roux in its iron pot

as I stir until my shoulder aches, the hidden
heat in carnation petals. And I love sex
so much, I believe the body does just fine

without ideas. Yesterday, an artist asked
for the story of my body. As her studio
skylight filled with snow, I remembered

a porch in late summer, and me, six or seven,
standing shirtless by the screen door,
feeling the glow of the whole day inside me

and thinking, *I want to remember this.*

I.

THEN AGAIN

While the world ends, burns, drowns, starves, I remember
summers at the house my mother rented in the country

outside Tuscaloosa, a two-story log cabin built by a judge
for his wife, two sons, and two daughters: two wings,

with connecting bedrooms upstairs in each, divided
by a high-ceilinged room with a fieldstone fireplace

where we spent nights reading—Tolkien for me,
Sayers or Christie for Mom. Sometimes out of the hush

came a staccato *click-click-click-click-click-click-click:*
wood-boring beetles, working their way through the walls.

"Killer invasives, just like kudzu," Mom said, but now I think
they'd always lived there. Late one autumn afternoon,

Mom came home to find the screen across the porch
slashed through, and shallow gashes in the doorframe:

a visit from one of the judge's daughters, who drove
from her apartment a few towns over to remind us

that she had grown up there and it was hers alone.
That first summer, Mom, tending her own grief

for her mother, often shut herself in her bedroom all day
while I wandered the surrounding woods, pines

swaying in the hot breeze, creaking and rustling,
making my neck tingle like someone was following me,

grit getting in my shoes, irritating my toes.
I'd circle back to the enormous yard gone half-wild

yet half-recalling its old blackberry brambles
and weedy beds of rosemary, marjoram, sage—

names Mom taught me. Back inside, I'd sneak
a few Nilla Wafers from the pantry, head upstairs

to reread *The Lord of the Rings*. One morning,
I dreamed the elves came to wake me in my bed.

Spread between us on my rumpled bedclothes
lay their rings, all three: their gift. "For me?

Really?" There they shone. "Yes," said the elves,
a little sadly. "We're done with them, you need them

more than we do." And they smiled somberly, watching
my hands rush through the sheets in whose furrows

the rings were lost as I woke, still searching.
Where do the worlds go we never held?

Maybe we'll just haunt whatever we can't imagine
comes after us—like me, now, emptying

my dehumidifier's bucket in my garden
at dawn, picking basil to flavor my eggs.

WHITE STONE

My windowsill's lined with fossils, white stone
remnants of lost oceans, lost bodies cast in white stone.

In the garden, I mutter *turmeric, borage, mustard, marigold,*
praying my name also takes root in time, in stone.

The beauty of rocks: weight, shape, a poetry of heft.
Stevens! I also cry, "Stanza my stone."

I lose the morning to arranging words, their meaning
now fainter than water on hot, dry stone.

My mother calls. Her neighbor was evicted, had to move
to another trailer, in another county—Limestone.

In my dream, I'm trying to call home
but the numbers fade into a pale, measureless tone.

Ammonite, echinoid, gastropod—you had no name
alive in your sea, only now when you are (why?) stone.

ZUIHITSU OF MY MOTHER'S BREASTS

As a child, I had nausea every time we drove back from crabbing and fishing on the piers at Dauphin Island. The corn dogs I'd washed down with Fanta, the prickle of cracked vinyl on the back of my sunburned legs, the smell of Coppertone mingled with my parents' cigarette smoke and the salt breeze blowing over me in the Rambler's back seat—our car's homeward motion churned it all in my stomach, despite the yellow Dramamine tablets my mother made me take.

Voyager 1 has now reached the heliopause. More accurately, as astronomers have learned from the data Voyager relayed, it has reached the "heliosheath depletion region," a transitional place, still barely "in the sun's magnetic embrace," as the article tells me. Galactic particles from interstellar space bombard it as it makes its slow, plutonium-powered way where we will never go. I say all of this in present tense, although I am aware that by the time the data reached us, Voyager had long since moved on. By now, it's probably slipped, no, lurched free, unbound—

cold, white sting of Solarcaine on sunburn: nothing could hurt us for long

The ashtray in my mother's car is always full. When we leave for the store, she lights up in the driveway, the air-conditioner going full blast against the scorching Central Texas heat.

All I remember of Büchner's play *Woyzeck:* the grandmother's tale about the orphan left all alone on the earth who went to the moon but it was rotten wood so he went to the sun but it was a withered sunflower and the stars were dead flies so he came back to the earth but it was an overturned pot so he sat down alone on it and cried and is crying still

every memory I've ever had: pulse from a dying star

She and I would walk the beach while my father surf-fished for flounder. We gathered scallop shells and sand dollars, but what I most enjoyed bringing home were worn slips of sea glass, their muted greens and blues. Back home, she dropped some in my bath so I could watch them regain their luster.

In 2011, as Voyager began its heliosheath exploration phase, my mother was again diagnosed with breast cancer; her first cancer, in 1983, was successfully treated with chemotherapy and radiation. This time it was not a reoccurrence but a new, very slow-growing cancer, also present in her lymph nodes. Because she had received such high doses of radiation previously, that treatment was no longer an option. She elected to have a double mastectomy.

Voyager's last step before entering the heliosheath was passage through the termination shock, "an environment controlled by the sun's magnetic field with the plasma particles being dominated by those contained in the expanding supersonic solar wind."

My mother's chemotherapy seems to have been successful. Her hair has grown back. She misses her breasts; I miss her breasts. She hasn't yet had her reconstructive surgery, and I'm doubtful that she will quit smoking long enough for the doctors to clear her for the procedure and the long recovery. When I see her, I see the shape her breasts made in her blouse.

the net hauled up at the pier's edge: crabs gnawing on chicken parts

Right after the grandmother's tale, Woyzeck comes home to his wife, Marie:
WOYZECK: We've got to go, Marie, it's time.
MARIE: Go where?
WOYZECK: Does it matter?
They go down the street.

My front porch is decorated with fossils my mother pulled from her yard, limestone trilobites and brachiopods slowly forced from the earth.

If Voyager 1 could feel, it would feel the interstellar winds.

ANTHROPOCENE VILLANELLE

The weather's beautiful and I'm still here.
Drought stunts my garden. I'd hoped for the best
because the forecast wasn't exactly clear.

I plant seeds, they sprout, then disappear.
The satsuma tree curls its leaves, distressed.
Still, the weather's beautiful. And I'm here,

along with dandelions that persevere
like aphids, squirrels and other pests.
Even if the forecast isn't very clear

for my kind, whatever's left won't need to fear,
with freeways to roam, our houses for nests.
Whither weather, whether wither . . . still, I'm here,

laying in flats of pole beans like last year,
picking wrinkled pods as if I've failed some test.
I blame the forecasts—have they ever been clear?

Indoors, I check my news feed, find my fears
gone viral. No putting them to rest.
The weather's fine, for now. I'm still here.
What's beautiful? *Nature morte?* Finally, it's clear.

THE GARDENER (I)

I dump coffee grounds and fruit rinds on the compost heap,
rinse muck from the bucket, scan the beds. Looking good,
except crabgrass has crept back around to irk the peppers,
and thistle's choking out that tomato. One row half-clean,
I glance at the flowerbed—what a mess, crowfoot
and nutsedge and a root-rotted lavender, last year's
failure, planted where heavy rains tend to pond.

Bushkiller's knotted in the kumquat and ligustrum,
snuck back in from the neighbor's side of the fence,
so I yank and grunt; later, fingers welted, I loop the vines
over one arm, bind the loop to itself, bag it. And still
that hydrangea hasn't bloomed, not in years, nor this
runty phlox, this blood orange blighted and barren—
I've lost hours, sunburnt, thorn-scraped, stuck here, outcast,
plucking this withered spearmint, sucking the tough leaf.

THE RAIN

for Tim

I need you to remember the rain—

lie down with me, love, and remember

all the rain we've known, while we know;

how it talked to itself through afternoons

like a boy with his imaginary playmate,

rain lost to itself in its coming, as we listened;

how it burst down morning lawns,

ending bright-beaded on castor bean leaves

and in your hair when you came in with the dog;

how the hurricane pelted through the porch screen

as we sat naked there in the after-dark, heat

heavy with wet, our slick skin one with night;

how sudden a fall—imagine you and me

loosened from the sky, oblate,

pancake-shaped, small wobbling

spheres cast down and finding

in falling one another, falling in air

as in one another, how, one body

spirited homeward, heavier

in falling further, we divide

to meet in earth again.

ODE TO BOWLS

Here's a nested set of five, tan, sturdy, rough-lipped,
my mother bought at a flea market from a weeping widower,

and there was once a chipped porcelain sink
where baby-I was bathed,

and a marble font where sinners' fingers dip—
but not mine, not in years.

I thought I knew the washbowl and pitcher, gold-rimmed,
my grandmother kept on a stand in my father's old bedroom—

heirloom, I thought, until, after her funeral, I pulled
from the pitcher's mouth a foxed paper tag:
2-piece, $49 50, in cursive pencil.

At the intersection of Jefferson and Claiborne,
I roll down my window to place five dollars
in a bowl a man holds toward me.

What is a bowl? Half a bubble
glowing, blown from molten glass,

clay thrown on a potter's wheel
then fired and glazed—

always fire in every bowl's making,
always a cooling to harden this soft shape.

In the kitchen,
I drape a towel over the bowl on the counter
where bread swells with a billion breaths,

I stack cereal bowls in a cabinet
like skulls in an ossuary,

and place, on the pantry's highest shelf,
broken halves of bowls I've loved
and might glue whole again.

There's the cats' water bowl
that says DOG.

There's the resin-lined bowl
that fills my head with smoke
I release like a prayer.

And here

is the bowl I live in,
reclaimed basin of a marsh

where Chitimacha hunters caught snipe for Creole housewives,
until the railroad came, tracing the basin's rim, then crossing it,

parcel by parcel marked off for houses, schools, libraries, streets
where potholes are bowls sand and gravel never fill

but water will.

ZUIHITSU ON THE LETTER *M*

Montréal: a guidebook on my desk. Whether to read it now, or when I arrive, or after I've been there.

Mucha: one of Mom's cats, but what did Mom really call her? She had a Mucha, years back. I'm trying it out now. Come, Mucha, come, kitty. The cat meows. Stretches a paw toward me. Skitters down the basement stairs.

Milk in a saucer every morning for Monkey, old black cat, little old man, her favorite.

Mulching in summer: sweet pine bark heat. Also, mealworms, mud, mosquitoes. Also, marigolds, mandevilla, and, every May, those red flowers over there.

Mart: small Texas town where my mother ended up. (How many moves since she was born? Dozens, plus a year-long post-divorce road trip, rarely mentioned.) Mart has its jail, donut shop, Dairy Queen (free WiFi), Pizza Planet, funeral home, all offering services I have never required. I have, however, been grateful for the police (hi, Chief Cardenas), Read's Food Store, Cozy Café (free WiFi), Catfish Hut (hi, Bobby), Dollar General, CEFCO

> and have stood at a country crossroad
> a mile outside of town, holding a scoop
> of Mom's ashes, looking for a place to leave them.
> Field? Fenced. Ditch? Disgusting. "Road,"
> said my uncle, pointing at the gravel
> and dust at my feet. "Always traveling."

Mom's money will pay for the trip to Montréal.
I have never been there.
Solely in that respect, it resembles my death.

Mycenaean Greek gave us **hermāhās,* which later became Hermes, my favorite god, deity of crossroads, poetry, and pranks. Also, a psychopomp. *Herma:* heap of stones, boundary marker. *Hermaion:* a lucky find. Mercury dimes!

Mom's jewels are driving me mad. Ali Baba's Carton, I've dubbed this box, smaller boxes and cases nested in it, ring boxes, bracelet cases, earring boxes . . . garnet pendants, this peridot crucifix, this orphaned diamond—but are they fake? beautiful? hideous? Who could I even give them to? I pack it all away. The Greeks imagined Plouton, god of wealth underground, a gaudier Hades, to mask their fear of death.

> Milkweed I've just planted and the nonexistent
> monarchs drawn to its nonexistent blooms.

M: from *mu,* from *mem.* Bilabial nasal. Double-humped, twin-peaked. Mood, memory, morbidity. Thickness of type. 1,000, and M̄, million. Male, Monday, Maccabees. \m/: metal salute. Meridian, matter, meter. The Messier catalog, 110 astronomical objects— star clusters, nebulae, galaxies. M-, Bantu prefix, *human, person, individual.* M1: Crab Nebula's remnant.

Medscape: "Myocardial infarction (MI) is the irreversible necrosis of heart muscle secondary to prolonged ischemia. Approximately 1.5 million U.S. cases annually." WebMD: "The starved heart tissue dies. This is a heart attack—"

> Starved heart! Oh, Mom!

II.

MATRILINEATION:
HOMAGE TO NELL PARKER (1944–2015)

I.

I'm trying to imagine you imagining me
finding, at the bottom of a plastic storage bin—

under clippings from your *Daily Camera* column,
under stray snapshots of family I never knew,
under rust-stained doilies and your baby shoes,
your life spread out around me on the floor—

this folder: "Confidential Materials Enclosed."

Your poems. I was, what, eleven? You took them out
to read to me, then burst into tears, ran to your study,
left them splayed beside me on the window seat,
summer light fresh as your mother's death that spring.

Imagine me finding your words, losing mine . . .

I know the typeface: that old Royal you gave me. And
"a mind that seeks / with words / to say these thoughts."

2.

"a mind that seeks / with words / to say these thoughts
that / wander as in a maze." I hear your heart—
iambic, broken. Rhythm, remains.

At your memorial in the Methodist church basement,
I read a few of yours aloud, should've stopped myself
from adding Williams, Dickinson, one of my own.
Suited, I sweated. Your brother wore a Marines tee.

Stories he told me: wild teenage-you, sneaking out
all night, then dating my dad. Stories your poems
from your second marriage tell: there was a woman
who acted like a wife. "I'd write you a love poem,

if I could. Instead, I've cleaned the house. I'd write
a poem that tells all the thoughts I have to share, but
rather put a clean ashtray by your favorite chair."

3.

You put a clean ashtray by your favorite chair,
read true crime, ignored the phone, smoked, smoked.

Three marriages left you happiest alone. The last
leeched your pension, but you reclaimed your name.

Were thirty cats too many? On my visits, their reek
choked my sleep. Sleepless, you ordered gems

from Jewelry TV to hoard in dresser drawers. (Appraised:
fake.) I found baskets of handed-down kids' clothes

you'd laundered for the next needy family. Checks
to the *Mart Messenger* to cover Catfish Hut's ads

when the owner's granddaughter was sick.
Regrets? None, you said, but: "I'd write a poem

if only I could say words that won't come out. Instead
I chafe and tease. Knowing that you know what I mean."

4.

"I chafe and tease"—I learn what you mean,
heartsick from what you learned in the edits.

```
Sometimes I think
I'd like to be a spy
and hid behind trees
and catch forty theives.
Sometimes I'd rather be a star
of Broadway shows
and buy my clothes
at a bazaar.
I've wanted to be
so many things.
Sought after by kings.
And when I've thought
of these,
I've been them in dreams.
And really, it seems,
that it's nice to be me.
There's no future in it.
```

5.

And really, what future is there but this
parsing of (y)our past?
       Thirteen sheets of typing paper,
8.5″ × 11″, 6″ × 9″, most dated May 1975.
Alone in a house deep in Alabama pines,
your husband away for work in Birmingham,
you used what you had. Grief left you time.

Clatter of keys all morning. A walk in the yard.
Weeding the garden, where you heard "a toad
setting-up shop by the tomato plants" and hurried
back inside to write it.
       Dad dropped me off in June
for the summer.
    You came out of your study,
gathered your poems, shut this folder
        I hold—
I can't—
   "Maybe I read too much. Mother always
said so. She's gone now, so I can't ask her why."

6.

You're gone now. And now. I can't ask why you wrote
"Confidential Materials Enclosed" across this folder,
like a spell to let you forget her, the one who wrote.

I can guess which poem you drafted last: scarred
with strike-throughs, felt-tip over typescript, "What is it?
What's wrong? . . . I scream, but make no sound.

~~Talk with me, touch me~~ . . . I could tell you things.
Why the search for Mr. Goodbar. A plug for
the emptiness. Let us pray . . . Watch the fruit fall

in on itself." You had to leave her there, with me
on that window seat, while you wept in your study.
You had to go on, with yet without her. She was

yet was not my mother. Years later, that line of mine
you said you kept rereading: *to be is yet to be imagined.*

7.

You said you kept rereading *to be is yet to be imagined,*
words that now come to me as if they were yours,
our words, together, apart from us, themselves.

"Complete within itself, my soul
becomes involved with trees
reaching silently toward the sun."

It's sunset. It's my birthday. I love sunset
and spending my birthday writing, all day,
and never having more than coffee gone cold,
an open dictionary, these trees going bare.

"I know the dishes are stacking themselves
in the kitchen sink. But, look, the berries
are turning dark. Let's go watch them."

This is me, imagining
                        you imagining me.

III.

THE PATH TO THE TG&Y

opens on the waste woods' edge, shallow, foot-worn rut
the little boy enters from Stein Avenue, coins' jingle

muffled in his pocket. Now he's halfway there,
at the minnow creek, where he lingers, knowing nothing

beyond trees and dappled shade, muted hum and growl
of traffic on McGregor, where he rode with his mother

the day the radio announcer broke, "Doctor King
has been shot." Mom's face snagged, taut:

what she felt, he couldn't name, frightened him.
Alone in these woods, he feels safe, this boy on his way

to buy a new rubber snake or Matchbox dump truck,
dawdling to scry the creek, beer can tabs and bottle shards

gleaming, without meaning.

If he could see years ahead, would he be stunned
by how easily I write "Doctor King has been shot,"

how the words slip like minnows through my thoughts
while the events stay fixed, stuck deep in time and earth?

He's lucky, this boy, to live in the past, in Mobile,
not here, in 2020, like my friend from high school

telling me about the Watertown cop
who bent her arm so hard and far up her back

to cuff her, cheek pressed against her trunk's icy lid,
she was glad her mother's fists had taught her mind

how to leave her body. Or a colleague who writes
about cops surrounding his car one morning

in his own driveway, hands on the steering wheel,
tie tied, suit fresh for work. I finish reading, get lost

online, researching, for a poem, details about a teen
a white vigilante shot, as if the flavor of Trayvon's last Skittles

would make his murder more real. More lyrical.

✻

                              The boy looks up

from the trash in the creek, drawn by the glare

of the strip mall parking lot through the trees. I'd lie
if I said he wonders why he never shares this path

with some other kids he's stood side by side with
at the TG&Y. There's one he's seen in a Batman shirt

by the action figures, and that kid in the creased jeans
wiggling a rubber snake—he knows him, can't think

of his name, doesn't try. (If he had,
could I conjure it?) I wish he would write down

their names, the toys they love. I wish he wondered,
Where do they go? Did I make them disappear?

NEXT DOOR

A woman checks her chicken coop at dawn
then posts the horror that she found: "Headless.

They were murdered." Cue the neighborhood chorus:
"What psycho does this?"   "Coyotes."   "Rats."

"Racoons?"   "A blue jay."   "Coyotes?"   "Decapitation
means someone, not something."   "Racoons will yank

birds' heads through chicken wire and chew them off.
Chickens have a gland they like."   "My money's

on coyotes."   "A sad state of affairs:
if one of us took personal responsibility

and shot a suspect creature, the police
would not applaud our reenactment

of Atticus Finch's honorable deed."
"I saw two on South Galvez last night."

"One dark, one tan? Our porch camera caught them."
Embedded in the growing thread, the clip plays

that loose-limbed trot, those down-sweeping tails,
their hurry to leave that harshly lit street.

"Free-roaming outlaw beasts."   "Last week in Chicago,
one killed a child by a nature museum. A child!"

"I'm hoping they stick around long enough
to cross paths with some window-smashers

and handle-pullers."   "That
would be justice served."

CONFEDERATE JASMINE

(New World Elegy)

Not true jasmine, love: star jasmine, woody liana,
trader's compass, soul's wheel, five fingers

of a merchant's proverb: *it shows the good man's way,*
my love, to white stars massed in shaggy vines

along our backyard fence, so many names chained
beneath the sky, broken alphabets crawling

like the blood of children through the streets
of home, the blood of children in our streets—

No, not true jasmine; truer: death
in our mouths at morning, mouths blind

as a ship's hold, blind to the words borne
in that slop and sludge, words sold for their perfume—

love, so many truths along our backyard fence!
When we bought this place, I hacked the vines

clear to their trunk's thick shaft near the ground,
and you said, *Jesus, how long has this been here?*

NEW ORLEANS LULLABY

Hush, everybody, stop your crying,
you'll wake the bullet that wants my baby.
Go to sleep, everybody, and when you wake
you'll have a circus with swans for horses.

In a vacant lot in New Orleans East
lies a bullet-ridden girl, still breathing.
Gnats and dragonflies veiling her eyes,
she whispers to the weeds for her sweetheart.

Her sweetheart's body lies cooling
in the morgue, bullet dreaming in his head.
When that bullet grows up, it wants to fly
like a horse in the circus.

Hush, people, I'm tired of your crying,
you'll wake the bullet that wants our city.
Go to sleep, people, and when you wake
you'll have a circus of murdered swans.

FIELD TRIP, BARATARIA PRESERVE

Ahead, between tupelos flanking the boardwalk that leads out of the swamp, a golden orb weaver hangs in its web, head down, its body as big as the hand of the little girl sobbing there, palms to her face, too scared to move.

       "It's OK, it can't touch you," I hear her teacher say, his fingertips on her shoulder, lightly guiding her. Her classmates' babble floats from the parking lot, where they've gone ahead to the bus. I could walk around her, but not while she's stuck here, rigid, alert, the spider high in the air barring our way.

       Alligators burrow into mudholes, egrets and blue herons roost. How can I go home? We're caught in the web of her terror's filaments spanning swamp and lowland prairie and the streets of the city where we live, as the sun sets and shadows drag the cold inland from the open Gulf. Did her ancestors, I wonder,

       hide here from men sent to hunt them for escaping? Unseen, some lived. Others, captured, their heads piked along the levee, live on in stories no one tells in school.

       She's calm now. She takes her teacher's hand and we all walk on.

    The web's threads sag.
    The spider waits.
    Night fills the forest.

WHAT IS THE FUTURE OF *UBI SUNT*?

Monday morning light on empty tables,
glinting on the legs of chairs I stacked
Friday evening so Harold could mop.

I'm looking over poems for workshop, thinking
about these students whose stories have just begun,
whose lives will be histories I'll never read.

Kindall writes of garden parties
pooled with beer and rank with blunts.
Her father's fingers bruised her throat
but couldn't choke her words back down.
She writes: "A caterpillar's first meal
is its eggshell." Nights after school,
she scans groceries at Breaux Mart
while she imagines pages for chapbooks.

A tornado smashed Taylor's house
but left her poetry books intact and shelved,
including the one she spent months making,
sewing photos in, binding its pages with yarn.
She danced step with Kindall freshman year,
is polite with white kids who say dumb shit
like "HBCUs seem kinda racist." "It's tiresome,"
she says, voice calm as a cloud on the horizon
before we start our discussion of *Citizen.*

Zeke taught *Moby-Dick* in pantomime,
playing Pip cast overboard in Stubb's rush to kill.
Pip adrift, head bobbing above water, watches
horizon's zero widen, "intense concentration of self
in the middle of such a heartless immensity."
Zeke flailed, circled by tables standing in
for the world's receding edges, eyes flashing,
hair floating as he sank and invisible boats

hunted their prey, leaving me to learn
daily I must watch, they must row
away from here to save themselves—

A bell, doors bang, stairwell voices swell.
I glance around the room before they arrive:
everything clean, as always, everything ready.

ONE FRIDAY AFTERNOON

New Orleans, June 2020

A tuba's thump and pulse
sends ripples through lockdown hush.

    A drum taps, a trumpet jumps in, calling me
    to stop refreshing pandemic data graphs
    and clips of George Floyd protests.

And, to honor my friend still recovering
from being hit in the head by a tear gas can
that did not exist, cops claim, so was not fired;

    to honor a high school friend's mother,
    a nurse, who died in a hospital bed
    one floor down from her dying husband,

I put on my mask, walk outside to follow
the brass band's blare to the house
whose porch is their stage. They are glad

    to see us—me, my husband, our neighbors
    Dean and Barb, Amy and Greg, moms
    with strollers, a pink-haired, pink-masked girl

and the friends who push her wheelchair.
We sway, dance, drop dollars in the tip bucket.
A silver-haired woman in a tie-dye dress

    steps closer, hands raised as the tuba player
    blows and sweats and the band swerves
    from "Liza Jane" into something none of us

has ever heard, this moment's answer to our need—

    a cruiser crawls by, lightbar flashing.

IV.

HOW ONE GOES ON

In the mornings, there is coffee.
Also, four cats, and a huge bromeliad
that has not bloomed in years.
In the mornings, there is the kindness
of the one who brought the coffee
and set it on the nightstand—let the day
wait while it cools. Over breakfast,
planes crash, flags fall, mothers die.
After breakfast, it is important
to be wrapped in a blanket on the couch
and coo "goofy girl" to the Siamese.
At noon, there is nothing to note,
just the memory of your mother reading
late at night with a cat in her lap.
One has no choice in these matters.
There lies the afternoon: it will be yours
until it isn't. Will you pick up the shirts
from the laundry, pay the bills, dig up
the daylilies from the now too shady bed
and move them to a sunnier one? (Five years
since you dug them from her garden.)
There went the afternoon: dirt
clinging to the bathtub, the checkbook
unopened on the desk, the kind one's
green shirt you love still unclaimed.
Here comes the evening, with its poem
you should have been writing all day;
evening, with all its unforgiven faces,
all yours. Night: dirt under your fingernails,
whiskey dulling your mouth, the box
of her pulverized bones on a closet shelf.
Where is the kind one? When will he be home?
Morning: as if it will never come.

NINE POSTCARDS

1.

I owe to the convergence of delayed appliances
and a myocardial infarction
this trip to Montréal.

2.

I keep seeing the same bridge and the same church,
beyond which, I have read, lies a body
of water with a name.

3.

That baby carriage is full of rabbits, black and white,
like the Holstein painted on a plate
in my mother's kitchen.

4.

Looking out from this mountaintop chalet,
I recall a ping-pong ball in Texas,
lost among daylilies.

5.

My mother, in STATION PLACE DES ARTS, was never confused
by exit signs pointing to and away
from RUE SAINTE-CATHERINE.

6.

On this seventeenth-century map, I can't find home,
just the word *Portage*—and there, below,
again the word *Portage*.

7.

This book tells me "*Il ne reste jamais assez de mots /
Pour mourir,*" but I don't know what that means
and I'm afraid to ask.

8.

My mother never told me about her late afternoons
watching the paddleboat riders
on the CANAL LACHINE.

9.

I have walked through the smell of the sea
only to cross train tracks
lined with cornflowers.

HOME

Two men, three cats, a dead dog's bowl. The dog's ghost,
under the dining table, licking and licking one paw.

A mother's spirit-forms: five—no, six—glass nesting hens,
two ceramic roosters (the smaller, it turns out, Portuguese),

a stout wooden hen and her chicks, each on wooden wheels,
ready to cart the mother's ashes down a Texas country road.

"So much clutter!" clucks one of the men, clearing the table,
junk mail in hand, books in the other, his mother's ashes

resting in his study and in the garden with one of her cats.
Under the bed, a suitcase of family photos, including a negative

of Bonnie and Clyde posing by a car on a gravel road,
like the one the mother's ashes traveled along one spring.

His mother and Bonnie shared a last name, and maybe now
they're sharing a smoke under a cottonwood, leaning

like a pair of wagon wheels against the side of an abandoned barn,
while he's at his desk with papers yet to be filed and folders

already full. "Where does it all go?" he asks, moving books
from chair to liquor cabinet to the floor by the tub, moving books

he examines but will never read, including the one he found
lying open beside her ashtray on the coffee table, the one

which spends its nights with the suitcase under the bed.

4 A.M.

And this sprained foot keeps me awake all night!
When will those pills kick in? Will they take all night?

Slumped in my reading chair, my leg's propped up, stuck
in a weird salute I'm forbidden to break all night.

Another episode of *The Walking Dead*—yes, skip the intro. . . .
Wish I had enough weed to stay baked all night.

I shift the ice pack, rewrap the bandage—it hurts
worse. What other pain will I remake all night?

Crutches, Oxy, doctor's bills piling up—
let's play the game called My Mistakes all night.

Some dumb thing I said rolls its ball of dung in my brain,
then buries it inside me, a brooding ache all night.

what art / Could twist—virgin feet—dread feet—did those feet—?
mind-forg'd collage of William Blake all night.

Touch the bottom of these sleepless hours? I'm
treading water in the middle of a lake all night.

Pain lights up my window
                         like daybreak all night.

"Brad? It's Mom. Sleep, baby." But you're dead,
so who keeps vigil for my sake all night?

TENANT

I don't believe in ghosts, haven't seen one
since I was three, peering over my bed's edge,

light from Mom's sewing room across the hall
catching the heavy shoes and taupe legs

of the woman who used to own our rented house.
I wasn't scared, didn't even think to question

why her legs were close enough to touch
while the rest of her lay under my bed

or somewhere else. I never told.
Mom's Singer rattled and throbbed,

paused, rattled and throbbed, and I fell
asleep and woke up here, grown old,

mother gone, grandparents, too many friends,
and the boy still there, safe in that light.

WAKING THE ANIMALS

Furred bone and muscle presses into my hand,
nudging me into half-light. Half-awake, I know it:
Freddy, my orange tomcat, beside me all night,

so I rub his head and scritch his chin
until a claw-tug from a dainty paw reminds me
Freddy's dead, over a year—this is Willow,

silly girl, always the first up, blue-eyed, hungry,
maybe the last cat my mother saw, as she lay
dying on her den floor. Then I stroke an ear

and a bent scar tells me this is Monkey, who begged
my mother morning and evening for cream, who begs
me morning and evening for cream. But this creature

feels tough: that brawler, Adam, terror of my teens,
a hunter dragging pigeons up the yew tree,
onto the balcony, and into my father's studio

just because he could, limping and growling
almost twenty years. He slept stone-still
(like me, dreaming now), so my father

would nudge him, ask: "Hey, are you alive?"

GREEN ANOLE

1.

I kept a lizard's skeleton
in a six-inch cedar box
I carried around the house.

I added a blue jay feather
and a nub of pink quartz
and wrote inside the lid—

I won't tell you what.
Tattered hide clung
to ribs and backbone.

2.

Crouched in grass,
I watched one perched
on a camellia branch,

eyes half-closed, sleek head lifted
toward the sun. Its dewlap swelled,
orange and pink against green.

I stretched out my hand
but already that body
was brown leaf fall, shadows.

3.

Muted yowl of a housecat,
small prey panting in its mouth.
The cat drops the lizard,

bats at it as it tries—
gut punctured, a leg
torn free—to pull

itself across the rug, past
its severed, wriggling tail.
Its claws snag in pile—

4.

I can't remember
the last time I saw one.
I click a link that tells me

the bark-brown subspecies
is making its way from Florida
and eating the green anole's eggs.

(A flood took my cedar box.
Now I can't remember
what I wrote in its lid.)

5.

I pull my car to the curb
to pluck a brown anole
from the windshield wiper

6.

and set it in the grass.

7.

Walking out to the porch
to get this morning's mail,
I saw the pale green body

clinging to the screen door.
When I walked closer,
my spirit flexed, unhooked

itself, and leapt
three feet with the lizard,
deep into sweet olive.

CRAFT TALK

for Carolyn Hembree

It must have rained last night:
my pineland mallow is blooming.

Pale yellow eye wide at sunrise,
it receives my image as I pass
on my way to pick parsley.

My pineland mallow's flower
looks like an okra flower,
and okra, too, is a mallow,
but not my mallow.

It doesn't mind
if you prefer the salvia's red tongues
or calendula's buttery suns.

Carpenter bees dip and suck
all day in blown oregano plumes,
in basil, germander, and gaura.

Slow mallow, it takes days
to make a green pod
silvered with whiskers.

Every morning,
one bee pays one visit
to this holy corolla.

"My *what?*"
asks my mallow.

"You should leave the garden,"
it tells me. "Go to a museum.
Have lunch with a friend.
Hasn't it been long enough?"

IMAGINE A WORLD IN WHICH
ALL MONUMENTAL LIONS ARE REPLACED,
EVERY ONE, WITH MONUMENTAL CHICKENS

I was at a birthday party in the Bywater
in a backyard with a stage, a wagon,
a cat asleep on a mattress in a trailer bed,
and three chickens roosting high up in a tree.

Between sips of champagne, we tilted back our heads
for a glimpse of those round, feathered darknesses—
OK, chickens, just chickens, but also
more like angels than the cat or us,

more like denizens of a sidereal coop,
and equally at ease twenty feet above the earth
as the Running Chicken, Lambda Centauri,
in its turbulent heaven.

I just ate a bowl of chicken stew
with turnips, carrots, rice, and collard greens.
I have no desire to eat a lion.
I could more easily befriend a chicken than a lion.

I do not want friends who are brave and strong
by dint of massive haunches and crushing jaws.
My friends don't lounge in the sun, licking blood-stained paws,
while I watch, pretending my fear is admiration.

My friends are busy. They spend all day
looking for what they need in the dirt around them.
They squabble. Have dust-ups. Stare, startle.
My chickens' nobility consists in their pertinacity

and their ordinary omnipresence
as domestic decoration—

this pair of Russian Orloffs, for instance,
giant frost-crusted pinecones on the library steps.

This modest flock of Transylvanian Naked Necks
posed on the four corners of Nelson's Column
ease the mind of imperial nostalgia
and offer no hope of empire's return.

Here is Richard, *Coeur de Poulet*.
Here is Christ, Chicken of Judah.
Here, in the desert, a man-headed chicken
crumbles away, never scratches toward Bethlehem.

And here is my mother, in her chickens
of green glass and of blue on my shelves,
and in her hen and rooster of cast iron
in the rain right now in my garden.

LAPIS LAZULI

for Dana Sonnenschein

Among all the unimaginable things, imagine
Shuggie Otis at seventeen,
composing "Strawberry Letter 23,"
playing three kinds of guitar, two kinds of piano,
also bass, organ, drums, and bells, and singing
every part, harmonizing with himself:

> *All through the morning rain I gaze, the sun doesn't shine*
> *Rainbows and waterfalls run through my mind . . .*

For four minutes and two seconds, I believe
there is no world without music,
without genius to compose and play it,
conjuring a garden where we sit and share
smoked trout and a white Bordeaux,
telling stories about the good in us.

The song ends; I play it again; nothing lasts
while we do. A quarter-million years of evolution
went into making Shuggie, and into our making
a quarter-million acres of New Mexico burn
and a million more tons of Greenland's ice
melt into acidifying seas; and theocratic thugs
place liens on every uterus; and a white kid
nursed on 4chan in pandemic lockdown
decides to save his race with lots of guns.

> *Blue flower echo from a cherry cloud . . .*

In my pocket, I keep a smooth nub
of lapis lazuli, tumbled and polished,
found at an herbarium in Philadelphia,

one more nub among hundreds heaped
in a basket, while the friend I was with
selected herbs for spells that keep her whole.
Later, we bought takeout barbecue
and ate it sitting on the sidewalk, amazed
to look at the crowded market we'd just left
and imagine it as it was a few months past,
as it might be again any day now,
locked, empty, its air no one's breath—

pitted gray flecks my fingers worry,
holy blue mottled with milkier hues,
remind me I'm still here.

V.

NAVIGATIONS

Surveying the porch tonight, I mark an aloe, an ivy,
last week's mail on a table, and wind chimes
fallen in a corner. Also, over my left shoulder,

a waning gibbous moon, and, south of my big toe,
the river that carried Huck and Jim, at this moment
gushing our homeland's toxins into the oily Gulf

while this story lights up my phone: a skeleton's
been extracted from the Antikythera shipwreck,
bones that might have belonged to the maker

of the first analog computer, a bronze orrery,
gears corroded, its two hundred teeth stuck
after two millennia beneath the Aegean.

It tracked the sun and moon into the future.
Well, here we are. Let the record show
our wreckage reflected the stars.

NO PITY THANKS JUST BUY THEM

In the market for sturdy footwear
for my imaginary life, I find
this ad tucked in the classifieds:
FOR SALE BABY SHOES NEVER WORN.
Perfect! I check my bank balance,
grab my phone, no number listed—

wait! I already know this story
and I cringe just seeing it
toddle toward me one more time:
I came, I cried, I died;
no one can fill those shoes;
if the shoe fits, you're dead.

My mother kept my baby shoes,
just like yours; just like you,
I've forgotten what carton they're in.
I guess she liked holding them—
how far my child has gone—
but she never had to know

nothing worked out and we're old,
in our ill-fitting suits of regret,
trying to remember, to imagine her
peering down into those shallow wells,
or graves, or little ears filled
with the silence of infinite space.

THE MAP

Last night I dreamed I grabbed a student—
nice kid who never shuts up—by his belt loops
and the collar of his jean jacket and hurled him
down the stairs. I woke in a sweat; today

I'm thinking it's time to move on. I have called
the secretary and she hopes I will get well soon.
I have allowed myself, with toast and coffee,
a shot of rye. The mind clears. A garbage truck

groans down the block and I brood on the days
I've missed its song, pent with twenty-six fiends
in a cinderblock, fluorescent-lit classroom
adorned with Scotch-taped quotes like *I was born lost*

and take no pleasure in being found. My neighbor
starts his yard work, pushing his push-mower
soothingly—*hush, chuckle-chuckle, hush*—
until his cranked-up leaf-blower kills this pastoral.

I really need to use those days piled up
like leaves or mail by the door, high time
I get far away. Farther: not Vegas, maybe Spain,
or I could blend in on a Holy Land tour. I'd need

candles, bug spray, cured flesh to chew. And cash
for the toll at the Martyrs' Bridge, the ticket
to the Martyrs' House, the tip for the docent—
no truth's revealed at a discount, friend,

least of all when you need it most . . . I need a map
but I'm a child who couldn't name the river
that never meant to drown him. And who's left
to imagine the river but the river's ghost?

MY DESIRES

OK, sure, I loved you,
parrot lily, princess lily, fancy-ass invasive
      stretching your spindly stems
above the sword ferns each spring,
      your blooms bristling all summer
until, spent, you went dormant,
      tubers swelling all winter,
dreaming the garden yours.

Now I'm almost rid of you,
prying out bits between border bricks
      and tree roots as I put in mallows,
wood sage, phlox, penstemon,
      natives of a garden I pray
you exiled from. Go on, get lost
      forever, you and your frilly friends.
I want what I want: not you.

CINDERELLA

Nineteen, I liked how tank tops, tight jeans, cutoffs
showed off my hundred push-ups, my lakeside runs.

Drag's magic wasn't mine, but it dazzled
when Dallas showed up to work à la Brooke Shields,

his chunkier, broad-shouldered body beguiling
as a girl I could get into. It was 1983. My world

seemed small, tidy, divided into men's and women's,
hits and misses. Dallas needed a wedding dress

for a show he meant to win, so after the tip-split
and shift drinks and ones for the road, we waiters

and busboys grabbed our go-cups and catwalked
to the fancy resale shop next door. The owner,

D's pal, had given him the key and her blessing,
for one night, to try on whatever we wanted.

"Girl, you're gonna rip those seams!" squealed Ray,
tugging at the zipper that refused to budge

another inch up D's back. "Godfuckindamn,
that was the *one!*" D squalled, shuffling off

the brocade-coiled gown he'd scoped all week.
Ray and the gang consoled him as they procéssed

into realms of lesser dresses. I lingered, seduced
by the gown that spurned D's girth; then stripped,

stepped into the sheath, reached behind, zipped.
"You *bitch!* And you not even a queen!"

No, never outside those walls, but as my queens
cooed, tugged and turned me for a crowded mirror,

I saw myself at fourteen, done up as Frank N. Furter,
a Rocky Horror party starlet, pert in thigh-highs,

garters, and corset; and see, at nine, I'm the star
of my solo closet dramas, raiding Mom's walk-in

when she goes out, some other body tingling
under flowy rayon prints, prince, princess,

so many suitors cloaked in their pursuits.

TALLOW TREE

Even the moon struggles to rise
from this invader's shaggy limbs.
I tried salt, have considered kerosene

poured one midnight over the fence
and onto the roots of my neighbors' tree—
not really theirs, this squatter, its seed

shit-borne by wren or sparrow,
its suckers and pods staking claim
to my garden plot, my lawful lot,

its shade stunting my satsuma,
its bulk blocking the view I had
years back from my darkened kitchen:

a second-story bedroom window
where, for a few nights, I watched
a young man standing as he fucked

an ass meeting his thrusts, so eager,
he and he, so relentlessly
alive,

stark as a flame-lit icon
of an Eden not mine
to lose.

THE GARDENER (II)

My grandmother laughed when I'd squat
while playing in the yard, poking a spoon

at the dirt, a little prissy as I plucked
fleabane's puny starburst blooms

to decorate graves I dug for pill bugs
whose armor coiled shut when my fingertip

pushed them under. They opened,
hauled themselves out. I wiped

my fingers on the grass. Hours later,
the smell of earth (or was it me?) lingered.

❧

My husband laughs when I come in for lunch,
boots muddy, knees caked, face smudged,

babbling—fritillaries! carpenter bees!
and we need more bags of soil

for the white sage and salvias I'll plant.
"Boots by the door, clothes by the washer,"

he says, ladling out bowls of gumbo.
I kiss his neck, inhale his spice, and again

fleabane's blooms turn to white-tufted globes
my breath blows bare.

ZINNIAS

There is never enough time to see everything
in the museums we visit most often.

I planted ten packets of seeds
and only these sprouted,

grew five feet high
and blew facedown in last night's storm.

Watching my husband chop an onion,
I think of all the poets no one reads.

Rooted in air, rooted in smoke,
washed away in silt-bearing floods—

"Don't worry, it's firm," I call out
to my four-year-old godson

as my right leg sinks to the knee
in the mound of dirt I'm climbing.

THE CROSSING

for Jim Richard

I've done this before: sidestepped
    down the bayou's bank with my father,
        stooping to help him slip the tarp

from our pirogue, easing it down
    to the water. I'm ten and this is magic
        while it lasts, our flat-bottomed glide

on the muddy current, dipping an oar
    now and then, just to feel the reason
        it was made. We pass willows

whose low-hanging branches trace lines
    on the surface, like my fingers dangling over
        the boat's low rim. We lull in the shade

of a river oak, six feet from a branch sagging
    from the weight of snakes piled asleep on it;
        some part of one of them rolls, another, slow,

unknowable knot—then one strand of the mystery
    stirs and wriggles free, ribbons down
        into shadowed water, then ripples across,

head lifted, past our boat to the sunlit
    other side. That's it; I'm here, I'm doing this
        until it can't be done, until there is no other

side, no farther to go, and no father,
    every loved, every feared thing stolen
        (as this boat will be in a month or so),

until I am equal to what the snake knows,
    slipping down from the tree, stepping down
        into bilge, head up to steady myself, pushing off.

HOW I CAME TO THIS

One morning I'm digging in the garden,
my shovel turning stalks of bolted lettuce
back into earth. Later, I'm shelving books
that have stood quietly in stacks for months,
sliding them back into alphabetical gaps
where I will forget them again for many years.
Chekhov in hand, I stop, thinking I heard the snap
of the raccoon trap shutting, but a glance
out the window says I'm wrong. Some other
morning, I'm listening to my husband's car
turn the corner as I open the notebook
on my desk and try to remember the line
I held in my head when I woke. By lunch,
I've read bad poetry and written worse, read
the news, signed urgent petitions and urged
you, my friends, to do the same. After lunch—
a roasted chicken breast, asparagus—I nap
until the orange cat walks over my chest
and I realize I have not yet left the house
and I realize I have no desire to. One summer,
I will dig an asparagus bed. I will read
all of Proust. I will teach myself the secrets
of extraordinary cuisines. This afternoon,
I read one page of a *New Yorker* and fall
back asleep to dream I am at the deathbed
of Gertrude Stein, in a group with the famed
chef Alice, and as Stein expires we all wander
out into the fields to watch the northern lights.
The cat walks across my grave, I mean, my heart,
again and I wake remembering that the lost line
contained the letter *l.* I could still make the gym,
or the library, or dinner, or another attempt
at a poem. Yes, all of that will be perfect
tomorrow, and perhaps worth talking about

later tonight when I greet my husband
on the porch with a glass of wine and ask
how his day was as I will ask him
every day for as long as we each shall live.

NOTES

"White Stone": The phrase "stanza my stone" is from Wallace Stevens's "The Man on the Dump."

"Zuihitsu of My Mother's Breasts": The quoted material describing Voyager 1's departure from the solar system came from an online news article which can no longer be retrieved. Much of the information can be found at NASA's Voyager Interstellar Mission page (https://voyager.jpl.nasa.gov/mission/interstellar-mission/). The lines from Georg Büchner's 1836 play *Woyzeck* are from the translation by Carl Richard Mueller.

"The Path to the TG&Y": I am grateful to my friends Greta Edwards and Maurice Carlos Ruffin for allowing me to share stories from their lives in this poem.

"Next Door": Mostly a found poem, with liberties taken, comprised of comments from the eponymous social media website.

"Confederate Jasmine": The lines "broken alphabets crawling // like the blood of children through the streets / of home, the blood of children in our streets—" are a paraphrase of lines from Pablo Neruda's "Explico algunas cosas" ("I Explain a Few Things").

"What Is the Future of *Ubi Sunt*?": I am deeply grateful to my former students for allowing me to share stories from their lives in this poem: Kindall Gant, Taylor Crayton, Ezekiel Martin.

"Nine Postcards": The lines "Il ne reste jamais assez de mots / Pour mourir" are taken from Mireille Gagné's book-length poem, *Les hommes sont des chevreuils qui ne s'appartiennent pas* (Montréal: L'Hexagone, 2015).

"4 A.M.": The italicized line borrows snippets from William Blake's "The Tyger," "The Book of Thel," and "Jerusalem."

"The Map": The quote "I was born lost and take no pleasure in being found" is from John Steinbeck's *Travels with Charley: In Search of America.*

"Cinderella": This is dedicated to my coworkers during the summer of 1983 at Flamingo's Café, New Orleans.

THANKS

To my father, Jim Richard; my stepmother, Rosalie Ramm; my husband, Tim Watson; and my in-laws: Myra Sands, Slade Watson, Nancy Watson, and Julie Watson.

To the teachers and students I have worked with, and to the institutions where I have been fortunate to teach: the New Orleans Center for Creative Arts, the Willow School (formerly Lusher Charter School), Louisiana State University, Tulane University, the *Kenyon Review* Summer Workshops, and the New Orleans Writers Workshop.

To Dr. Joe Willis and Dr. Christopher Dunaway of the Louisiana State University Agricultural Center's Louisiana Master Gardener program, and to my fellow students of the class of 2022. Special thanks to Susan Goss and Tammany Baumgarten for helping me identify a mallow.

To Dana Sonnenschein, for years of friendship, critique, and support. May we have many more.

To the members of my workshop group of many years: Katy Balma, Allison Campbell, Peter Cooley, Toi Derricotte, Carolyn Hembree, Rodney Jones, Laura Mullen, Kay Murphy, Andrea Young.

To Ron Mohring and Seven Kitchens Press, for invaluable support of LGBTQ+ poets.

To James Long, at LSU Press, for his encouragement and support; to Ashley Gilly, whose brilliant copyediting clarified and brightened many of these poems; and to James Wilson and the Press's design and marketing teams for their exceptional work.

To the reading series and festivals that have sustained me and my community: the 1718 Reading Series, Blood Jet, Dogfish, Lucky Bean, Poetry Buffet, Rubber Flower Poetry Hour, the Splice Poetry Series, the New Orleans Poetry Festival, the Tennessee Williams & New Orleans Literary Festival, the Saints & Sinners LGBTQ+ Literary Festival, and the Words & Music Literary Festival. Also, the reading series at the University of New Orleans, Tulane University, and Xavier University.

And to Karren Alenier, Tom Andes, Morgan Babst, David Baker, Susan Bernofsky, Julia Carey, Nicole Cooley, Tracy Cunningham, John Davidson, Karin Davidson, Jarvis DeBerry, Anna Duke Reach, Tonya Foster, Anne Gisleson, Erick Gordon, Anya Groner, Chase Greene, E.Gross, Kelly Harris-DeBerry, Megan Holt, Hundreds Brass Band, T. R. Johnson, Jessica Kinnison, Susan Larson, Cameron Lovejoy, Ed Madden, Kerrin McCadden, Emily Moore, Lara Naughton, Alison Pelegrin, Lynn Putney, Maurice Carlos Ruffin, Alex Scalfano, Adrian Van Young, Nancy White, and Paul Willis.

☙

I am grateful to the editors of the following publications, in which the poems listed first appeared, sometimes under different titles or in slightly different forms: *Bayou Magazine:* "Zuihitsu on the Letter *M*"; *Cleveland Review of Books:* "Next Door"; *Cortland Review:* "Then Again"; *Crab Orchard Review:* "Confederate Jasmine"; *Fugue:* "New Orleans Lullaby"; *Gettysburg Review:* "The Crossing" and "How I Came to This"; *Green Mountains Review:* "Matrilineation: Homage to Nell Parker (1944–2015)"; *Hypertext Magazine:* "Zinnias"; *Laurel Review:* "How One Goes On"; *MockingHeart Review:* "Nine Postcards"; *New World Writing Quarterly:* "Craft Talk," "Green Anole," "Imagine a World in Which All Monumental Lions Are Replaced, Every One, with Monumental Chickens," "The Map," and "The Path to the TG&Y"; *Nola Diaspora:* "Field Trip, Barataria Preserve"; *Okey-Panky:* "The Rain" and "Zuihitsu of My Mother's Breasts"; *On the Seawall:* "Anthropocene Villanelle"; *Plume:* "White Stone"; *64 Parishes:* "The Gardener (II)," "Navigations," and "Tenant"; *Southern Review:* "How I Am Whole"; *Tahoma Literary Review:* "Ode to Bowls."

The following poems also appear in the chapbook *In Place,* selected for the Robin Becker Chapbook Series (Seven Kitchens Press, 2022): "Cinderella," "The Crossing," "Green Anole," "Home," "How I Am Whole," "How I Came to This," "How One Goes On," "The Map," "Next Door," "Ode to Bowls," "The Rain," "Then Again," "What Is the Future of *Ubi Sunt*?," "White Stone," "Zinnias," and "Zuihitsu of My Mother's Breasts."

www.ingramcontent.com/pod-product-compliance
Lightning Source LLC
Chambersburg PA
CBHW021646150125
20426CB00002B/127